ZOLTAN
THE MAGNIFICENT

Bob Graham

Happy Cat Books

Jack never saw much of his Dad, who left early for work and got back late at night. Sometimes Jack got up to see his Dad. 'Never enough time,' said Dad, and was gone.
Just a cold teabag left behind on the kitchen sink.

But on the night before their holiday it was different.
His Dad was home for dinner.
Just when he thought Dad wasn't looking, Jack showed the entire contents of his mouth to his sister Grace.
Dad just sat there with his fork in the air — dark as a storm.

The steam drifted slowly off Dad's spaghetti
and fogged up one window of his glasses.
Jack laughed. He couldn't help it.

But Jack's Mum didn't take it too seriously.
When they were alone in the kitchen she took
her rubber glove with the fingers inside out and blew.
'Holidays tomorrow,' she said.
Jack thought Mums were definitely more fun than Dads.

'Tell me, Jack,' said Dad at the start of their holiday.
'Tell me you haven't just given Grace's dummy
to Leo,' and he tapped his foot with irritation.
'I haven't . . .' said Jack.

Mum helped.
To the tapping of Dad's foot she sang,
'My Baby's gone and left me,
and I am feelin' blue,
I'm feelin' oh so lonesome . . .
. . . Do de do de dooooo!'

'What's "do de do" mean?' said Jack.
'It means I've forgotten the words,' said Mum.
'It goes something like,' said Dad,
'Don't you love me, Babeeee,
Don't you love me too?
Rock it with me, Babaaay,
And I will rock with you.'
'Dumb song,' thought Jack,
but sometimes his Dad surprised him.
'Let's get on the bus,' said Mum.

Their bus arrived at the hotel late in the afternoon,
with the harbour strung out before them —
the smell of the oil and the smell of the salt, and
the low thud of the sea heard from their hotel window.

'Let your father sleep,' said Mum.
'He's had a long journey.'
Jack's lip dropped and he played
with his rocket launcher . . .

. . . which landed a plastic missile
almost up Dad's nose.
Then Dad went very quiet.
'Watch it, Jack,' he said.

That night they had dinner in a restaurant.
'For a special treat,' said Mum.
Jack did not like restaurants, even on holidays.
He just sat there not wanting to move
in case he knocked over his water
or used the wrong fork or knife.
He need not have worried because it was Grace
who provided the action.

She should never have been given peas.
Off they went, rolling across the floor.
But this time Dad wasn't angry.
He just pointed at the peas with his fork and said,
'They've made an escape bid.'
'What?' said Jack.
'They're trying to get out the door,' he said,
'before Grace eats them!'
Was that a joke? Jack looked at his Dad.
Dad was smiling. It *was* a joke.

The first day of their holiday, the sun shone
and Grace shone with sunscreen oil.
Freckles appeared on Mum's nose.
There were other children.
The cold water took Jack's breath away.

He ran up the dunes to lie on a hot concrete roof.
When he got up to Repel the Invaders, there was
the wet dark shape of him, drying in the sun.
Like leaving his shadow behind.
'Shadow Man,' said Jack.

Jack picked Mum for his tunnel trick.
'Mum is just about OK for this sort of thing,' Jack thought.
'Dad could be . . . difficult.'
The canvas of Mum's chair snapped tight under her
weight, and she swung gently over Jack's tunnels.

One tunnel too many and the back of Mum's
chair slowly subsided into the hole,
tipping Mum and her glasses sideways.

'Shadow Man strikes back,' said Jack.
There was a slight delay while Jack decided
that Mum was in fact going to smile.
Surprisingly, he saw Dad laughing too.

And surprisingly, Dad said, 'Cover me with sand.'
He lay there with sand stuck to his face,
a racing car driver hurtling across a desert.

He moved even faster when Leo came to make his mark.
Jack thought his Dad was sometimes fun.

They spent the next day on the rocks.
Jack found his own special rock pool.
He stood like a giant in his underwater garden.
Leo took tentative sips of salt water,
and Mum collected shells with Grace.
Dad set a trap for tiny fish.

The family were horrified.
'Dad, you're not going to put those sweet
little fish on your fishing line . . .?'
'. . . ARE you?'
'Err, of *course* not,' he replied,
'I just wanted you to see them,' he added,
'then I'll put them back in the sea.
I shall use some cheese on my hook, of course.'
'Good old Dad.'

'We don't need a TV,' said Dad that night,
'*or* the rocket launcher. We shall
make our own entertainment.' Jack's mouth drooped.
'I give you . . .' said Dad,
'. . . the Award-winning, the Fearless, the Incredible,
Animal Trainer Extraordinaire, ZOLTAN THE MAGNIFICENT.'

'You will see, ladies and gentlemen, boys and girls,
that this animal, wild and fearsome, from the jungles
of deepest Africa, will leap through my arms (a human
hoop, ladies and gentlemen) in a single bound.'

But all the Wild Beast could see was an ear being
offered to him, like a soft pink shell.
His little tongue darted in and out.
'Not in the ear,' said Dad, 'through the hoop.
Through the hoop.'
Jack thought his Dad was OK.

When the sun wasn't shining Dad said, 'Let's go to town.'
They bought pancakes with a double serve of ice-cream.
They went into a little booth with a curtain,
to take their own photos.
Mum arranged her hair to look beautiful.
When the flash went off, Grace and the Wild Beast
looked surprised, Mum was smiling nicely, and Dad
was pulling an even sillier face than Jack.
The machine gave them a strip of photos.
Mum looked at them and silently shook with laughter.
Jack had never seen his Dad look like that before.

Next day it rained and the sea washed high on the beach.
'Shall we look for treasure?' said Mum.
'YES,' they all replied. 'What sort of treasure?'
'Treasure left behind by the sea,' she said.
'Pieces of eight from a pirate's chest . . .
or silver and gold. Pearls in the shell.
Or a stranded mermaid,' she added.
'I have walked many times on stormy beaches,' said Dad,
'but never have I found a stranded mermaid.'

'I usually find one of these.'
He held a rubber flipflop in the air, white and
bleached by the sea.
'I think there are a lot of sailors out there,' said Dad,
'with one shoe missing — one shoe fallen overboard.'
'You're joking with us, Dad,' yelled Jack.
'Zoltan to you,' said Dad.

Jack took the rubber flipflop and placed it
on the window ledge of their hotel.
'Just in case you find the other one,' said Mum.
'Or maybe you'll see a fisherman with
only one shoe,' said Dad.
'It certainly doesn't belong to a mermaid,' Mum added.
'They only have tails.'
That afternoon at the wharves, Jack and Grace appeared
more interested in the fishermen's shoes than in their boats.
'I'm sorry,' said Dad. 'Our children are a little too inquisitive.'

On the last night they climbed a hill overlooking the water.
'Imagine,' said Jack, 'that we are all sitting in
the nose cone of a massive rocket . . .'
'. . . about to blast off into space,' said Dad.
'With a bit of help from your rocket launcher,' added Mum.
'With Mum at the controls,' Dad went on.

'And Zoltan the Fearless here in the engine room,' said Mum.
'Magnificent . . .' said Jack. 'Zoltan the *Magnificent*,
and I can be captain, and the Wild Beast can repel invaders.'
'What about Grace?' Dad asked.
'I don't know,' replied Jack.
'Maybe we can find some sort of job for Grace.'

Now they are home and Dad is working again,
but most nights he is home early.
He can hardly wait to get his coat off.
He kisses Mum, Jack, Grace, and Leo —
and most nights they play the rocket game.
They all take turns to hit a missile into the salad bowl,
except for Grace and Leo.
Mum is the champion. She calls Dad a 'trier'.
Occasionally he scores a point and the family applaud.
Dad says, 'Perhaps we can all go back next year
and find the other flipflop, *or* the one-legged fisherman.'

'And perhaps by next year,' said Dad,
'the Wild Beast will be tamed
and going through the hoop.'